The door was opened by a stout, motherly lady with a kindly twinkle in her eye.

"Goodness gracious!" she exclaimed when she saw Paddington. "Whatever have you got there?"

"It's not a *what*," said Judy. "It's a bear. His name's Paddington and he's coming to stay with us."

Paddington

TAKES A BATH

MICHAEL BOND
illustrated by John Lobban

HarperCollins *Publishers*

From the very beginning it was clear that Paddington was the sort of bear who couldn't help getting into a mess.

When he first arrived at the Browns' house he was covered in jam and cream and Mr. Brown had to give the taxi driver some more money.

"Bears is sixpence extra," said the man. "Sticky bears is ninepence!"

"Just wait until Mrs. Bird sees you!" exclaimed Judy. "She's a bit fierce sometimes, but I'm sure you'll like her."

"I'm sure I shall if you say so," said Paddington. "The thing is . . . will she like *me*?"

"Mercy me!" cried Mrs. Bird. "I haven't put clean sheets in the spare room or anything – though judging by the state he's in perhaps that's just as well! I think he'd better have a bath straight away."

"I've had an accident with a cream bun, Mrs. Bird," said Paddington, as Judy led him upstairs for a bath.

"Where did you say you came from?" called Mrs. Bird.

"Darkest Peru," replied Paddington.

"Hmm!" said Mrs. Bird.

"Then I expect you like marmalade. I'd better get some extra supplies in."

"Fancy her knowing I like marmalade," said Paddington, as Judy led the way towards the bathroom.

"Mrs. Bird knows everything about everything," said Judy's brother, Jonathan.

While Jonathan got the bath ready, Judy explained matters to Paddington.

"There's one tap marked hot," she said, "and one marked cold. Here's a cake of soap and a clean towel. Oh, and there's a brush, so that you can scrub your back."

"It sounds very complicated," said Paddington. "Couldn't I just sit in a puddle?"

"I don't think Mrs. Bird would approve of that," said Judy. "And don't forget to wash your ears. They look awfully black."

"They're meant to be black!" exclaimed Paddington hotly. ". . . I think."

After Jonathan and Judy had left, Paddington peered at his ears in the mirror. He decided that perhaps they were rather black after all.

Luckily, there was a tube of white stuff on the washbasin, so he was soon able to put them right again.

After that, Paddington tried writing his name on the mirror, but it was much longer than he'd expected and he soon ran out of tooth paste.

He was beginning to feel hungry again, but the cake of soap Judy had given him didn't taste like any sort of cake he'd ever eaten before. In fact, it made him feel rather sick.

Unaware of the problems Paddington was having, Jonathan and Judy got ready for tea in the room below.

"I do wish Paddington could stay for good," said Judy. "He's all alone, and London is such a big place if you have nowhere to go."

"I daresay," said Mr. Brown, "but I still think we ought to report the matter to someone. Anyway," he added darkly, "it all depends on Mrs. Bird."

Just then the door opened and Mrs.
Bird herself came in. Everyone went
very quiet as they waited to see what
she had to say.

"I suppose you want to tell me
you've decided to keep that young
bear?" she said. "I must say I'm very
pleased. He raised his hat, and I like
bears with good manners."

"Fancy that!" said Mrs. Brown,
after Mrs. Bird had gone. "Whoever
would have thought when we left
home this morning that we'd end up
having a bear living with us!"

"Hooray!" said Judy. "I can't wait
to tell Paddington. Just as soon as
he's finished his bath. . . ."

But far from finishing his bath, Paddington hadn't even started yet. He was too busy drawing a map of Darkest Peru on the bathroom floor with some of Mr. Brown's shaving cream.

In fact, he was so busy, it wasn't until he felt a trickle of water run down the back of his neck that he realised the bath was full of foaming water.

He tried looking for the taps, but he couldn't find them anywhere.

And when he stood up again, he couldn't see the bathroom either!

In the end he decided there was only one thing for it – that was to jump in!
But he soon discovered it's one thing jumping into a bath . . .

. . . but it's quite another matter getting out again, especially when the sides are slippery and your eyes are full of soap. He tried bailing out the water with his hat.

Then he called out "Help!" – at first in quite a quiet voice so that he wouldn't disturb anyone, then in a much louder voice. "HELP! HELP!"

"That's funny," said Mr. Brown, "I could have sworn I felt a spot of water."

"So did I," said Jonathan.

Judy jumped to her feet, pulling Jonathan after her. "Come on!" she hissed.

"What's up?" asked Jonathan.

"It must be to do with Paddington," whispered Judy. "I bet he's in trouble again."

"Are you all right, Paddington?" called Judy.

"No!" cried Paddington, "I'm not! I think I may be going to drown."

"Gosh!" said Jonathan, when he saw the state the bathroom was in. "What a mess! Even I've never made a mess like this."

"Oh, Paddington!" said Judy, as she and Jonathan helped him out of the bath. "Thank goodness you're all right. I should never have forgiven myself if anything had happened to you."

"It's a good job I was wearing my hat," said Paddington.

"Why on earth didn't you pull the plug out?" asked Jonathan.

"Nobody said anything about that," said Paddington. "I wish I really had sat in a puddle now. I shall never, ever, have a proper bath again."

All the same, when Paddington came downstairs again everyone had to admit that he was looking much, much cleaner than when they had first met him.

Mrs. Bird brought in a fresh pot of tea and a large pile of marmalade sandwiches, and in no time at all things were back to normal.

But before he went to bed that night Paddington had one more go at having a bath, only this time he made sure the taps were turned off.

"It's what's known as a *dry* bath," he announced. "It's safer than using water, and it's much less messy."

Carnival is an imprint of
HarperCollins Publishers Ltd
77-85 Fulham Palace Road,
Hammersmith, London W6 8JB

First published by Carnival 1988
This edition first published 1992

Text © 1976 Michael Bond
Illustrations © 1992 HarperCollinsPublishers Ltd

ISBN 0 00 192624 1

Printed in Great Britain by
BPCC Hazell Books, Paulton and Aylesbury